'AS LIKES APPLES AND EGGS

82

KNOWLEDGE BOOKS

MASTERY DECODABLES

Tas is a cat.

She likes a pat.

She likes apples and eggs.

She likes to play, play, play.

Her mat is a toy.

Her mat is her bed.

Tas is so kind.

She is so good.

She is so little.

Tas likes me.

Bes is a bear.

Bes is a toy.

Tas likes Bes.

Tas is a pet.

Bes is a toy.

Bes is so little.

Tas and Bes like to run and play.

Tas and Bes like to sit.

Bes and Tas are so tired.

Tas and Bes like to sleep.